Parents and Caregivers,

Stone Arch Readers are designed to provide enjoyable reading experiences, as well as opportunities to develop vocabulary, literacy skills, and comprehension. Here are a few ways to support your beginning reader:

- Talk with your child about the ideas addressed in the story.

- Discuss each illustration, mentioning the characters, where they are, and what they are doing.

- Read with expression, pointing to each word. You may want to read the whole story through and then revisit parts of the story to ensure that the meanings of words or phrases are understood.

- Talk about why the character did what he or she did and what your child would do in that situation.

- Help your child connect with characters and events in the story.

Remember, reading with your child should be fun, not forced. Each moment spent reading with your child is a priceless investment in his or her literacy life.

Gail Saunders-Smith, Ph.D.

STONE ARCH READERS

are published by Stone Arch Books
a Capstone Imprint
1710 Roe Crest Drive
North Mankato, Minnesota 56003
www.capstonepub.com

illustrated by
Andy Rowland

Library of Congress Cataloging-in-Publication data is available on the Library of Congress website.
ISBN: 978-1-4342-2508-5 (library binding)
ISBN: 978-1-4342-3049-2 (paperback)

Summary: Gary wants a pet. Which one will he pick?

Reading Consultants:
Gail Saunders-Smith, Ph.D.
Melinda Melton Crow, M.Ed.
Laurie K. Holland, Media Specialist

Art Director/Designer: Kay Fraser
Production Specialist: Michelle Biedscheid

Printed in the United States 3908

Little Lizard's
NEW PET

by Melinda Melton Crow

STONE ARCH BOOKS
a capstone imprint

This is Dad Lizard.
This is Mom Lizard.
This is Gary Lizard.

Gary wants a pet.

"Look at the dog," said Gary.

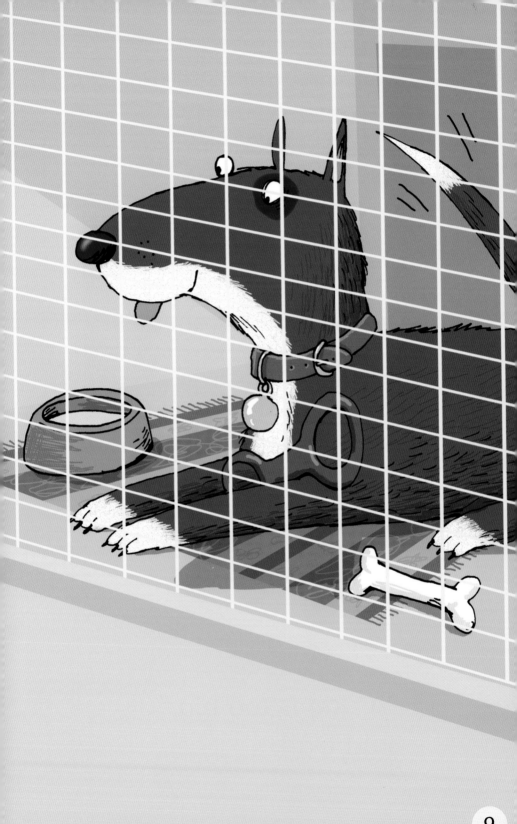

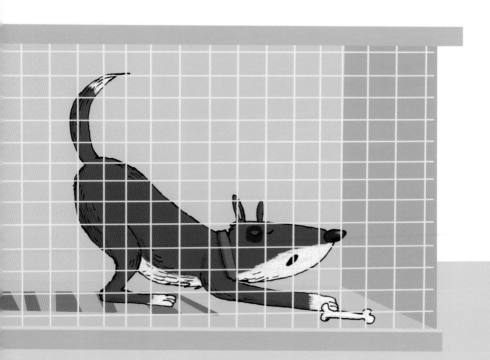

"A dog is too big,"
said Dad.

"Look at the cat," said Gary.

"A cat is too big," said Mom.

"Look at the fish," said Gary.

"A fish is not too big,"
said Dad.

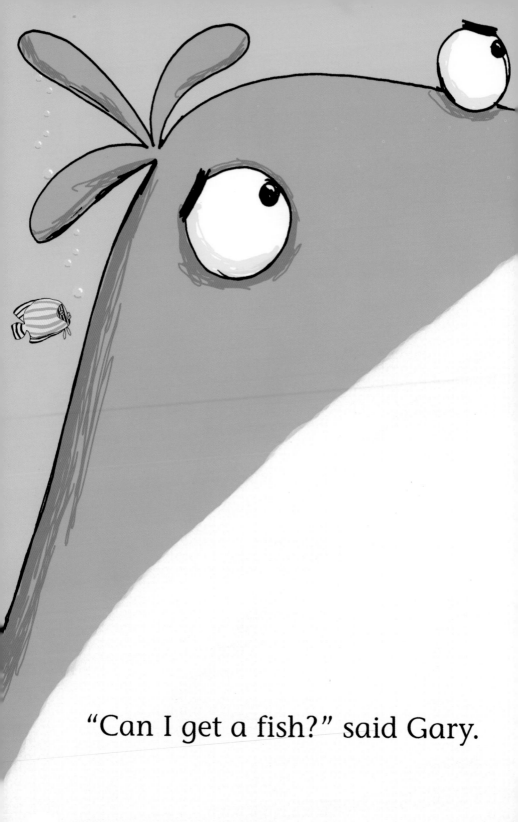

"Can I get a fish?" said Gary.

"Yes," said Mom.
"Yes," said Dad.

"Oh boy!" said Gary.

"A little fish for me,"
said Gary.

"A little fish for you,"
said Dad.

"A fish is a good pet," said Gary.

STORY WORDS

lizard	dog	fish
pet	cat	little

Total Word Count: 95

Little Lizard's BOOKSTORE

STONE ARCH **READERS** LEVEL 1
Little Lizard's
NEW FRIEND
By Melinda Melton Crow

STONE ARCH **READERS** LEVEL 1
Little Lizard's
NEW BABY
By Melinda Melton Crow

STONE ARCH **READERS** LEVEL 1
Little Lizard's
NEW SHOES
By Melinda Melton Crow

NEW TITLES